Zana the Brave

by: L.K. MaSon

DEDICATION

I dedicate this book to all of the strong, phenomenal women on whose shoulders I stand. My Mother, Laura R. Mason, has been my first teacher, supporter, encourager and example of a woman's devout love and strength. My love and appreciation for her can't be captured with words. In addition to my Mother, there are a number of women who were motherly figures at some point in my life that don't even realize what an impact they had on the path of it: Grandma Kathryn Bell, Edwina Whitehead, Margaret Hightower, Laura Cooper, Selena Pruitt, Betsy Wise, Lorayn Hughley, Elaine Small, Jennie Johnson, Cindy Hugley, Brenda Hill, Brenda Smith, Diane Gary, Ruth Sewell, Lorraine Freeman, Charlotte Julian, Patricia Moore, Daisy Williams and Judi Toles.

Although the following beautiful souls are no longer with us, the love I felt from each of them still lives within me. In honor of their memory, I dedicate *Zana the Brave* to my grandmothers Thomasine Wise-Mason and Florence Allen, my aunts Emma Jones, Flora Allen, Cynthia Gene Mason, Mamie Cayson Hunt and Martha Allen and to other motherly figures also gone to Heaven, Myra Hugley, Elizabeth Cotton, Geraldine Manson, Sharon Grayer, Lela Strickland, Wanda Benbow, Edna Pincham and my fifth grade teacher, Mrs. Martin.

I can't forget my sister-friends that without their encouragement, friendship and support through some tough times as an adult and young adult, I don't know where I would be: Mary "Cookie" Newell, Debbie DiVencenzo, Cynthia Little, Bobrea Robinson, Monica Kirkland, Nakia Cayson, Christina Robinson, Andrea Heflin, Carlisha Miller, Misty Lemon, Marla Smith-Bercheni, Taniishaa Wright, Sherry Grayer, Darlinda Smith, Jeni Crowe and Keeshia Rowe. I'm also truly grateful for my Aunties, Darlene Allen, Florence Manns and Priscilla Renee Johnson, for being everything aunts are supposed to be and more. Thank you to Paulette Edington for her unconditional support, my LaBrae High School English and Spanish teachers, Mrs. Johnson and Mrs. Ortiz and one of my college instructors who gave me the nickname "Miss Do" because of all of my hairstyles, Attorney Kim Akins.

Finally, I dedicate *Zana the Brave* to all of the bullied little girls hanging in there in the midst of ridicule. This book is dedicated to the bullied little girl that lives within me and the little girls living within many women who endure and may still be in the process of overcoming fat shaming, body shaming and other forms of bullying specific to women. Most importantly, I dedicate the book to my future daughter of whom I have dreamed since I was a child and to the memory of my beloved brother looking down on me from Heaven, Vincent Allen, Sr.

Zana the Brave

Written by: L.K. Mason

Cover and book illustration by: Qin Mobley

Bonus coloring page illustrated by: Kamilah Thomas

Edited by: Monique Matthews

Layout design by: Julia White

www.ZanaTheBrave.com

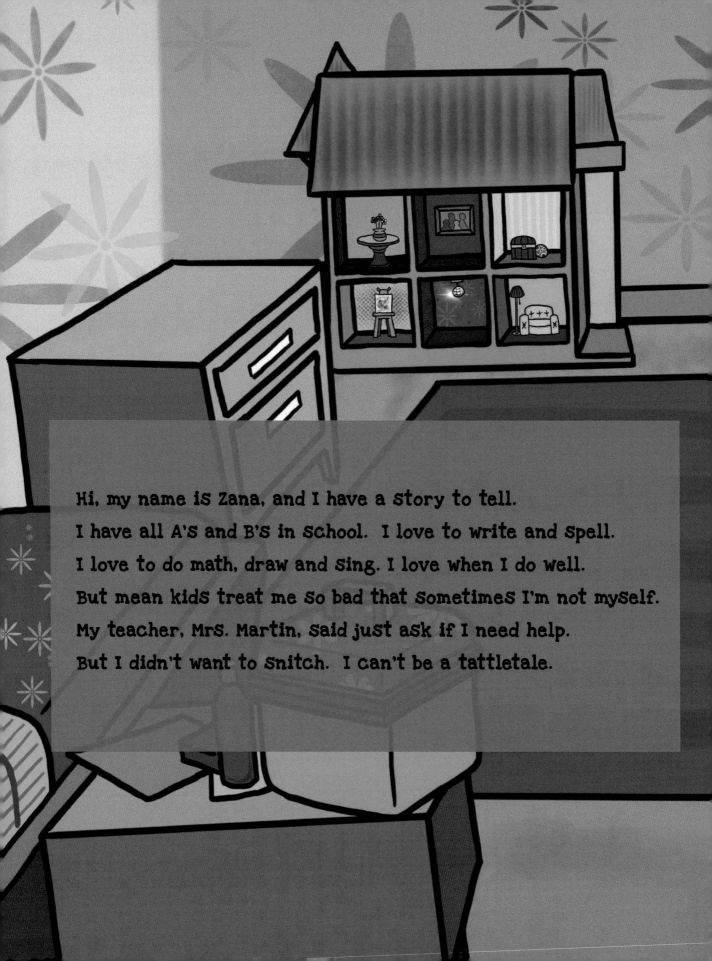

Hi, my name is Zana, and I have a story to tell.

I have all A's and B's in school. I love to write and spell.

I love to do math, draw and sing. I love when I do well.

But mean kids treat me so bad that sometimes I'm not myself.

My teacher, Mrs. Martin, said just ask if I need help.

But I didn't want to snitch. I can't be a tattletale.

I don't know why kids pick on me. I think I'm pretty cool.

I talk to everyone in class. I never pick and choose.

Yes, I'm taller than some classmates and bigger than some too.

But I'm not that much bigger than them. It's not like I am HUGE. They call me bad names every day. I hate to go to school. I hate being called fat pig or cow. I don't know what to do.

The mean twins, Amber and Autumn, are giving me the blues.
They're pretty with good hair. The boys think they are cute.
Unless you wear the hottest styles, these girls won't talk to you.
One day they bullied me during lunch right outside the school.
They pulled my hair and pushed and shoved and even kicked me too.
All because Jace likes me, they like Jace, but Jace has no clue.

Jace is the popular captain of our basketball team.

He's also my best friend and lives next door to me.

We're very close. We've been best friends since we were two or three.

He doesn't like Amber and Autumn. They're mean, and he's so sweet.

I don't know how anyone likes them when they're both so mean.

I've got to get out of here, so they can stop hitting me.

I'm not afraid of either of them. I just don't like to fight.

I warn them to stop before I tell. But there's no teacher in sight.

There's two of them and one of me, but I'm not going to cry.

"How do I bust out of this corner?" That's all that's on my mind.

So, I yelled loud "GET OFF OF ME," and ran with all my might.

The principal called their parents. They said sorry like ten times.

It's not just me being bullied. My friends also get teased.

Miguel is picked on daily and called a computer geek.

Kids say Karlie is black as tar and that she has big feet.

And Jace is called an Oreo but not the kind you eat.
Bullies tease me when they're in crowds. They point and stare at me.
They laugh because I'm pigeon-toed and also I'm knock kneed.

Johnny is the worst bully. He bullies us all the time.

He doesn't listen to teachers. They can't keep him in line.

Students are scared to stand up to him. He's much bigger in size.

He once punched me in the stomach and said he had a knife.
I told my Mom. She told his Mom. But Johnny always lies.
His Mom always believes him. So, they never apologize.

I told Mrs. Martin about the things that go on before school.

"Mrs. Martin, Johnny called me fat and stepped on my new shoes."

She said, "How can he call you fat when he's much bigger than you?"

"Just tell Johnny that you can lose weight. But he will never be cute."

She said, "Beauty's not just what's outside. It's what's inside of you.

You're not only pretty outside, you're beautiful through and through."

They say you have to exercise. That's how you'll lose the weight.

I already do exercise. I play outside all day.

I'm a kid. I eat what I'm fed. Adults still fix my plates.

What do I know about calories and carbs? Just let me go and play.
I'm too young to stress about bullies or the size of my waist.
Why won't people just leave me alone? Why won't they go away?

When we're away from home, I see people stare at my knees.

And because I'm pigeon-toed, kids point and laugh at my feet.

It's much better when I'm at home, and everyone knows me.

I have lots of fun with all my friends that live right down my street.

We play kick ball, tag, volley ball and even hide and seek.

Our mothers make us all play outside. We can't just watch TV.

One day, I wasn't playing. My brother saw tears in my eyes.

He asked what's wrong. I had to tell. I dare not tell a lie.

He said, "You're brave. Stand up to them. I taught you how to fight.

You cannot let people tear you down and mess you up inside.

You have to be happy and feel safe. You have to live your life.

Meet the bully after school tomorrow, and I'll be by your side."

I told my brother, "I've got this. I know just what to do.

You can't fight this one for me, Vince. You have to turn me loose.

I know bullies are scary with really bad attitudes,

But you taught me to defend myself and that's just what I'll do.

You can't be there in the morning when doors open for school.

I'll figure this out on my own if the bully gets cruel."

I texted my friend, Karlie, "Hey, I have a masterplan.

That bully's going down tomorrow. Help me if you can."

I sent her a few text messages spelling out the plan.

If we do this right, Johnny won't soon mess with us again.

She said, "I've got your back, Zana. We're friends until the end."

I said, "Get there nice and early. Don't forget to blend in."

I looked in the mirror that next morning and practiced what to say.

Johnny, the bully, will be waiting, pointing and calling me names.

I got off the bus and walked to the front steps where students must wait.

And there he was surrounded by his crew. He walked over my way.

I said, "Look, Johnny, just leave me alone. Today is not the day."

He said, "SHUT UP," and shoved me hard, so I yelled "STOP" loud in his face.

I said, "NO MORE. Don't touch me again. Boys shouldn't hit on girls.
Touch me again, and I'll hit you back and make sure you see swirls."
He grabbed my hair tight, pulled it hard and knotted up my curls.

Karlie leaped from behind the bush and threw down her fake pearls.

She held up her phone still filming as Johnny spun in whirls.

His face hit the ground so hard it was heard around the world.

Karlie got it all on tape, and Miguel broadcasted it live.
He hacked the TV in the teacher's lounge. We knew they'd be inside.
I finally caught Johnny in the act so this time he can't lie.
His eye was swollen like a bubble, and this he can't deny.
Johnny got a text from his best friend that he should run and hide.
The teachers saw the video, and they're all coming outside.

He grabbed his eye. Then, he yelled at me, "I'll get you. You just wait."
I said, "If you put your hands on me, you'll suffer the same fate.
I don't know why you bully people or why you're filled with hate.
But if you keep on messing with me you're going to learn today."
He said, "whatever. Let's go guys." They turned and walked away.
The other kids dabbed on them and called me "Zana the Brave."

The principal called our parents. My Dad came by to meet.

They talked about Johnny and how I knocked him off his feet.

Johnny was suspended from school for the rest of the week.

I didn't get in trouble because he was bullying me.

Dad held me tight, said he was proud and kissed me on the cheek.

Kids outside held up signs saying "Zana the Brave's our Queen!!"

I like that name. Zana the Brave. But I really don't like to fight.

I don't like hitting at all. My Dad said to always be kind.

But sometimes you must defend yourself. You can't be scared and hide.

I won't be quiet while kids are bullied. I cannot just stand by.

I will speak up. I am not scared. My Dad taught me wrong from right.

Zana the Brave will save the day when there's a bully in sight.

ZANA THE BRAVE THANK YOUS

There are so many people I need to thank for their unwavering support and devotion to my vision for the ***Zana the Brave*** book series but none any greater than God. God blessed me with the purpose, the talents and gifts to create something so powerful and giving. My vision doesn't end with this first tale of ***Zana the Brave.*** My prayer is that this book ignites bravery, compassion and kindness deep within the hearts and minds of our youth as well as the adults serving as role models in their lives.

Children inspire me to do better and be better, so I hope that I get to reciprocate that inspiration through the voice of Zana.

I recall the moment I knew I was ready to write this tale. I was creating logos with the incredible illustrator of this book. The way he was able to take my written and verbal instructions and visually bring them to life exactly the way I envisioned them simply amazed me. It was as if I had an epiphany. I visualized him and I making that same magic happen within a children's book. Feeling disheartened with the all too often news reports of youth taking their lives or shooting up schools and realizing that many of these incidents could be traced back to bullying or ostracizing, I felt I had a responsibility to share my experiences. I endured and overcame bullying and constant teasing about my weight and being knock-kneed and pigeon toed as a child. No child should go through that feeling that they are alone. I believe writing about it in a picture storybook with images to captivate the children could change or save someone's life. So, I told the illustrator that I was thinking of writing it and would love to have him do the artwork. He accepted and less than a year later, we were working on ***Zana the Brave*** together. Thank you, Qin Mobley! I could not imagine anyone else illustrating this series with me. You have marvelously created a brilliant picture of my dream.

I often tell friends, family and fellow writers that I don't like writing if it feels forced or planned. I prefer to let the inspiration hit me and let the words flow through me as if I am just a vessel through which the words find their way to paper. This method held true as I wrote the first draft of the manuscript of ***Zana the Brave.*** Believe it or not, after thinking about what parts of my life I wanted to lend to Zana's life, I wrote the first draft in less than two hours. I immediately sent it to close family and friends asking for feedback. Without hesitation, when I showed them the manuscript, they asked how they could support my dream. It is undeniable that God was ordering my steps. I had only asked for their feedback. They generously gave me their time, money, free services and more. Attorney Billi Copeland – King, Jacquelyn Golden, Erica Ziegler – Roberts (web designer), Toyiah Marquis (publishing advisor), Monique McGee (marketing), Kevin Smith (marketing), Gregory Jackson, Sr., and Nova Phoenix, thank you for your support and obedience to God.

In addition, my immediate family has been my backbone helping me every step of the way throughout my writing and publishing process. No matter how I needed them, they were there. So, with everything that I am, I thank you, Mom (Laura R. Mason), Dad (Rev. Calvin H. Mason), and my brothers (Robert Allen, Calvin M. Mason, Anthony Mason and Denzel Stevens). I also have to give a special shout out to some of my nieces, nephews, and little cousins (Abraham Crowe, Nathaniel Crowe, Aniyah Allen, Zy'ionna Allen, Ca'lin Mason, Camren Mason, Cay'cee Mason, Ka'Niya Cayson and Akilah Thomas) for being the first youth to read and share their opinion of my book. Thank you to an incredible young artist, Kamilah Thomas, for illustrating the BONUS coloring page at the end of the book. A host of other relatives and friends helped by simply being excited for me and proudly wearing ***Zana the Brave*** merchandise. I love each and every one of you. THANK YOU!!!

Last but not least, I must thank my wonderful editor, Monique Matthews, for joining my Brave Circle. Thank you for challenging my writing, pushing me to more clearly depict my vision and believing in me.

ABOUT THE BRAVE AUTHOR

Photo by: Shamecka Nelson

L. K. Mason has always had a love of writing. Writing poetry and rhymes has been one of L. K. Mason's favorite pastimes, from elementary school through college. She was often labeled a "teacher's pet" or "brown-nose" because English, Writing and Spanish teachers and professors marveled at her writing abilities. Her essays and term papers were often read aloud in class as examples of how a work should be properly written. So, it wasn't a surprise to those that know her that she would write a book.

L.K. Mason obtained her Bachelor of Arts in Business Administration at Kent State University. In addition to taking classes, she tutored students in several at-risk programs including Upward Bound and Kent State's KEEP program, all while working full-time at a child welfare agency. While continuing along the path of her mission to impact the lives of youth and devote time to community service, L. K. Mason was also an Executive Board Member alongside Kevin and Kim Stringer for the nonprofit youth outreach program they established in honor of their brother, Korey Stringer, upon his untimely death during training camp with the Minnesota Vikings. Additionally, L. K. Mason served as liaison between Grammy award-winning singer, Usher Raymond's, management team and his fan club, The Usherworld Fan Club. Witnessing her obvious passion for youth empowerment, Usher's team invited her to volunteer at Usher's New Look Foundation, the singer's annual two-week business camp centering on sports, music, dance, videography and acting.

Subsequently, L. K. Mason was tapped to join the team of Tyrese Gibson, Grammy-nominated singer and actor in the *Transformer* and *Fast and Furious* movie franchises, among others. With Tyrese, L. K. Mason has worked on two books. She conducted research, transcribed and formulated questions for his New York Times best-selling book, *Manology,* co-authored with Rev Run of the famed hip hop group, Run DMC. She also contributed to Tyrese's yet to be released self-improvement book, *Black Rose.* In addition, L. K. Mason organizes, facilitates and moderates media press conference calls for Tyrese including those with artists on the rise and his A-list celebrity friends such as Lee Daniels. She has assumed many duties working alongside Tyrese besides media press conference calls such as recruiting on-location staff, composing and handling business correspondence emails with fans, prospective business partners, corporate America and international multibillionaires. The most satisfying outcome from the many responsibilities she assumes is the positive impact on all the lives she touches.

Even in the midst of battling with debilitating medical issues that impaired her ability to be as hands-on and active in the aforementioned movements and previously mentioned opportunities for several years, L. K. Mason still strives to make a difference in the lives of youth. The heartbreak it caused when she wasn't healthy enough to accept offers to move to Los Angeles and become the success she had always believed she'd be was almost as detrimental to her health as her illnesses. It was more frustrating and depressing than the constant testing and doctor's appointments. She had to undergo lumbar punctures to remove excess cerebral spinal fluid due to a condition called pseudo tumor cerebri and take a strong anticonvulsant medication that causes her to sleep or be extremely lethargic most of the day due to a condition called trigeminal neuralgia. L. K. Mason channeled her frustration and confusion about her illness into her writing as a way to release stress and attempt to have some sort of normalcy in her life. The disability made her even more determined to be an example to youth that not only can you overcome bullying, if you never give up, you can make it through anything even heartbreak and health issues.

The trajectory of all of these experiences led L. K. Mason to writing **Zana the Brave,** her latest and most exciting endeavor to date. As her health permits, she aims to diligently strive to take the **Zana the Brave** series and franchise to heights greater than she can even imagine.

Made in the USA
Columbia, SC
25 March 2020